Verses and Tales

Published by : Notion Press

First Edition, 2024

ISBN: 979-889632643-4

Price: ₹199.00

Printed in India

Verses and Tales

MOMENTS OF WONDER

AARNA KHIVASARA

For my father,
who never stops believing in me.

PREFACE

"I love writing. I love the swirl and swing of words as they tangle with human emotions."

— James Michener

The Little Things in Life: A Pocketful of Poems, was my debut effort in writing poetry. In this book, I embark on a journey that intertwines storytelling with the art of poetry. This is my first foray into the world of storytelling. The tales, born from my imagination, resonate with the nuances of our contemporary world. Through these pages, I invite you to explore the depths of human experience, emotion, and the complexity of life. I hope you find this book a delightful and enriching reading experience.

I would be glad to receive your feedback on *aarna.khivasara@gmail.com.*

Cheers!

Aarna Khivasara

CONTENTS

VERSES

Mindful Musings

Stories in Stanzas

Inspiring Introspections

TALES

VERSES

VIVID VIGNETTES

JOY

Joy spreads with a grin,
From a godsent friend.

It sounds like laughter,
Like fairy tales with happy ever- afters.

Joy flutters like a fairy,
Spreading bright light.

It feels like a long weekend,
Or a long holiday to travel the globe.

Joy glistens like a little raindrop,
Twinkling as if on display.

It smells like steaming samosas,
On a lazy, rainy day.

Joy sparkles like a snowflake,
Delicate, pretty and crystalline.

Joy tastes like a lollipop,
Dollops of ice-cream or cold sips of lemonade.

Joy is a freshly baked muffin out of the oven!
And the smell of grass, the roar of waves.

For me, joy is this poem,
Black ink, filling up white paper!

LUXURY

Richie, Rich, Rich:
That's what luxury is for most.
Mansions, private jets, holiday homes:
That's what luxury looks like to most...

Fresh currency notes, aroma oils and perfumes:
That's what luxury smells like to many of us.
Silk tapestries, wall hangings, and pretty hand fans:
Luxury feels like golden dust!

Lavish meals, sumptuous feasts and fine gourmet:
That's how luxury tastes, isn't it?
A hundred servants thumping up and down staircases,

a jingle of gold every now and then:
That's how luxury sounds —bells of heaven!

Or does it really?
Not for me.

A chat with a friend, a good day at school;
Popcorn with a game of carrom.
A sizzling pizza straight from the oven:
That's luxury for me.

Warm bubble baths and a cosy warm bed:
That's how luxury feels like to me.
Chocolate ice cream and cotton candy:
Luxury tastes sweet to me!

My parents' pep-talk, my brother's giggles:
That's how luxury sounds like to me.
A roof above my head, a cosy bed, a loving family,
That's what luxury means to me!

BEING SILLY

How does being silly look like to you?
To me, it feels like sticking out my tongue and saying 'boo'!!

How does being silly feel like to you?
To me, it feels like singing aloud in the loo!

How does being silly seem like to you?
To me, the world's most ridiculous jokes with 'knock-knock-who'!

How does being silly sound like to you?
To me, the sound of endless hiccups, and loud burps too!

How does being silly taste like to you?
For me, extra sugary biscuits with lemon-euww!

How does being silly smell like to you?
For me, a whiff of raspberry toothpaste and
syrup of mayonnaise-double for you!

How does being silly look like to you?
The reader of this super silly poem – you!!

JOVIAL JOTTINGS

EXAMS AND DREAMS

'Pens down!' The teacher cried
'Hurray!' we shouted in reply
And indeed, I must admit,
Our faces had never looked so lit.

For at last, after what seemed like forever
We were done with our exam fervour!
After an eternity of feeling unnerved,
We felt what freedom felt like to caged birds!

Oh, the joy felt on the chiming of the school bell!
Oh, the bliss of not being shut in that classroom cell!
Nothing can beat the ecstasy of going out to play and dance

That thrill of dumping the books and not sparing them a glance.

When you can walk around without a book stuck to your nose,
Stop reading pages of endless prose.
Oh, the happiness that bursts from the children's hearts,
'Exams over... over at last!'

And then, out of the blue
Pulling me back from what seemed too good to be true
I heard a shout. 'What?' I said,
As I got out of bed.

Oh no, no, no, it's Monday,
My first paper is TODAY!
Can anyone make me forget my dream?
There's a long way to go before joy beams!

SOLEFUL SHOES

Pointy shoes, gum boots,
Tippy-toppy-topple-shoes.
Handsome-leather-soled-boots —
What'd you like to try?

High heeled, strappy shoes,
Springy-silly-smiley-shoes.
Aesthetic dance shoes —
What'd you like to buy?

Shiny shoes, long boots,
Try-not-to-topple shoes (phew!).

Flip-flops-that-look-funny (euww!) —
Would you dare to try?

Sporty shoes, smart boots,
Silver-sparkly-shimmer-shoes.
Lovely-long-leather-boots —
That's what I'd love to buy!

HAPPY HILARITY

A HISTORY EXAM TOMORROW

I have a history exam tomorrow,
I pull out my textbook and scramble through my papers
I bury my head in that sea of antiquity,
Fearing, my braincells may vanish into vapour.

I have a history exam tomorrow,
I flip through, trying to cram it all in my little brain
Emperors, invaders, revolutionaries and so many mortals
There's so much to learn, I wonder if I'll remain sane...

I have to study, oh dear!
Can I bully my brain to learn these hieroglyphics?
Tomorrow, I'll be freed from all the artefacts and relics.
I just can't wait for my mind to be clear.

What battles did the British fight?
When was the World War over?
Who dropped the first missile?
I can't cram the dates anymore —

I open the first page, there's no time to laze,
I must study, I make up my mind,
But from the window, I steal a gaze,
A million reasons to take a break, I find.

Which was Napolean's last battle?
Why was Jhansi so well guarded?
Who used the first gun barrel?
And the French Revolution who started?

I must study and I resolve that I will,
In my own creative way,
Concocting a history of my own,
It's manageable, this way...

I might not score well tomorrow,
I did not study as much but wait!
'The exams are postponed by a week due to rains.'
The notice uploaded by the principal said!

'Yippee!' I shouted in ecstasy. 'Time to play!'
I surely was smart to *not* study today!!

A BACKWARD DAY

Today, I've had the weirdest day,
I woke up in the night and stayed wide awake!
I brushed my teeth with cotton candy,
On listening to jokes, I became unhappy!

I put my socks onto my ears,
And when I was scolded, I loudly cheered.
I wore my clothes inside out,
Read my books upside down.

I studied for the test after getting full marks,
Tried to find my shadow in the dark.
I played hockey with a tennis racquet,

Didn't pay for the grocery shopping in the market.

I ignored my friends, played pranks on teachers,
I drank my soup after cooling it in the freezer.
I tried to stand up on my head,
And took a nap under my bed!

I tried dying my hair green,
I didn't follow any routine.
Finally, when the day was through,
I smiled and thought, 'Tomorrow, let's try something new!'

Does this happen to you anytime?
Do you also feel like acting weird?
Is this a thing about growing-up?
Is this sudden rush of emotions to be feared?

EXAM FEVER

Tomorrow's my first exam,
I'm trying to act cool.
Tomorrow... my first exam —
I just can't wait for school!

I know the test will be difficult,
The answers won't be known.
I'll scratch my head —
I'll wish I had a phone.

I'll have to study, go through notes,
Work out math.
Learn a lot—
There's no escape from that!

I know I'll be exhausted,
I know the ordeal.
Studying will be a nightmare—
Exams are a big deal!

Will I go mad,
Or will I remain sane?
Has all this study tossed my braincells—
Outside the windowpane?

Wait, I think I have a fever,
A sore throat, a bad cough or a bout of cold.
Is it pneumonia or malaria—
I ought to rest lest it gets any worse.

Exams will come and go,
But I am my dad's lil' girl, you know.
So, it's better to give the exams a miss—
Snuggle inside my comforter and rest, what bliss!

NATURE'S NOTES

AN ACORN IN THE SNOW

Like a snowman in boots,
I was walking in the deep snow,
But stumbled and fell onto an oak's frozen roots,
And spotted an acorn lodged in the snow.

Brown, shiny and hatted, it lay covered in frost:
In the winter wonderland, it was lost.
I wondered, which chipmunk dropped its food?
Which oak tree did it belong to?

I walked on, for my destination called out to me.
But I just couldn't leave behind that fallen seed —
I picked it up and ran my fingers across it, snow soaked.
And gazed up at the tall leafless oaks.

And whenever I wrap my summer fingers —
Across that autumn trinket, feeling forlorn,
Something inside my heart stirs and whispers,
And the air suddenly smells of brown acorns.

It was just an acorn,
An acorn in the snow.

Cold, snow-soaked and shiny —
An acorn in the snow.

GOLDEN RAIN

Last night, I closed my eyes,
And in all the darkness—
The world was mine:
But—

It was raining,
And the rain was golden!
And the world clambered to be—
A part of my dream.

The raindrops singing a melody,
And clouds playing the drums—
And the fluttering leaves playing the notes:
Oh, what a beautiful tune!

Freshening the lakes, streams and brooks, it babbled,
And mellowing the yellow grass, it pattered.
A smile played on everyone's lips,
A song in each heart.

Then I awoke and peeked outside,
It was just a wild dream.
It was raining, though,
Glistening drizzling rain—

Do I crave the rain of gold—
Or the golden rain?

What is more life giving—
Gold or the rain?

Maybe one day we shall—
Smile at younger kids and say
'We yearn for the gold in the rains,
For that is real wealth.'

And look up to the Lord and pray,
'Thank you, oh Lord,
The diamonds are pretty but not quite a bargain—
Nothing can beat the Golden Rain.'

MINDFUL MUSINGS

ONE GOOD TURN

A sparrow pecked at my window one day,
I smiled, made a place for it to nest and stay.
The sparrow looked at me, with grateful eyes
As if to say…
Thank you!

Far away, a child was lost in the woods one day,
A little sparrow flew to her, chirped and showed her the way.
The child looked at the birdie, with grateful eyes
As if to say…
Thank you!

Is this the way the world goes, I wonder —
One good turn begets another!

THE STARS STILL SHINE TONIGHT

I look up at the starry sky,
Sparkling like a Princess' crown in the ball,
But what I see is way beyond it—
Beyond it, in the World of War.

I see the stars shining bright,
Lighting up the velvety night.
I hear explosions of bombs far away—
Cries of agony for the loved ones lost.

Bodies every inch of the ground,
Smoke obstructs the sight.

Yet, standing here in safety—
The stars still shine n' smile tonight.

Winter's gone; spring arrives:
Flowers blossom, birds sing their song.
Happiness and warmth reign—
But not in the World of War.

Not for those who are fighting,
Not for those nations torn by war—
Not for those broken hearts:
No, not for all those innocent lives lost.

I look up at the starry sky,
Wishing, Lord, let there be no more war—

Because when all the wars of our world are over,
The night's embers would not care if no one found them aglow—
Those ancient sentinels will always shine:
Distant dreams of joy, against the velvety night.

War will bleed us, hate will tear us all apart,
Wars will come, wars will go.
Let the spring of love blossom in every heart—
Let the light of humanity glow.

CHILDHOOD

As silly as a hiccup,
As sweet as candy.
As cosy as a warm water tub—
And as lovely as a beach so sandy.

As cute as a teddy bear,
As busy as a bee.
As naughty as my little bro—
And as adventurous as the wide, swelling sea.

As sparkly as a smile,
Or water rippling in the pool.
As pure as a melody on the lyre—
Or the mischievous giggles of a child in school.

As noisy as a baby's rattle toy,
As smiling as a smiley.
As dear as your favourite soft toy—
And as warm as a muffin baked nicely.

As kind as a fairy godmother,
As thrilling as a roller coaster ride.
As playful as a baby—
And as innocent as a child.

Foolish yet wise, carefree yet responsible—
What more do you expect from a child?
When the skies are full of stars and dreams and light,
When those blossoms are wonders, and the
butterfly her guide,
When the swing swings her right into the sky—
And the world is a wonder, and the child learns what is life.

Life has many seasons,
Autumn, the rains and summer and spring—
But the most beautiful of them all, I believe,
Is the one I'm in.

Oh, childhood is spring!

When the blossoms are wonders,
And the butterfly my guide!

FOREVER

The rippling of waves on a sandy shore,
The smell of fresh grass—
The tinkling of breaking glass,
A gushing waterfall.

The sparkle of a sister's smile,
The gold of a Christmas star—
Tales of a Godmother's miracles,
And of the genius genie.

The coziest blanket I've snuggled in,
A never-ending candy from my dreams—
My mother's gentleness,
A mermaid divine.

Books taking me along to faraway places,
The aroma of baking brownies—
The hug of my parents, my brother's laughter,
The love of family.

There are some things that we can never forget,
Dreams we've dreamt, wonders we've witnessed—
Beauty we've known, love we've felt,
Wishes we've wished, hopes we've cherished.

Some memories never fade,
I won't forget them, ever—
They will stay etched within me...
Within my heart, forever.

STORIES IN STANZAS

THE PRODIGY

When The Prodigy comes to school,
It'll not be a day to miss.
Don't be absent—
Don't pretend you're sick.

In the maths lesson while you sit feeling bored,
Brains swim, eyes close.
When the teacher cries out—
'What is the answer? Anyone knows?'
The Prodigy gives out a shout.

'I know! I know!
It's $77x^2+55x+64$!'

Which sounds Greek to your ears,
Like 'I know all the answers, you can doze!'

The math lesson is gone in a blink—
With a couple of happy snores,
But the Prodigy makes the teacher believe—
How well the students can score.

In chemistry, you wake up and close the math book,
And sorrowfully pull out the next.
And while the teacher is demanding formulae of radicals,
You dream of places miles away.

'What are the atomic numbers of silver, gold and platinum?'
'I know! It's 47 and 79 and 78!'
The Prodigy is at it again—
What does she eat? What makes her so sane?

And the chemistry lesson is gone in a daze—
Silver and gold and all metals fine.
While what you dream of, are silver jewellery and golden cakes,
The Prodigy and the teacher work on their formulae.

The English teacher walks in,
With intentions to give the hardest spelling test she can.
You look at The Prodigy, your hopes are high—
'This too shall pass,' you sigh.

And The Prodigy works her magic—
She makes the teacher explain,

All the vocabulary instead.
And so, the Dictation lesson is sorted.

In history, you snap out of your daze—
As the teacher threatens you with dates and deaths,
You feel dull, tired and depressed,
And long for a break.

So as the teacher drones about conquests and battles and kings—
And how the World Wars created unrest,
Your beseeching eyes plead,
'Please, give US some peace instead.'

And soon enough, the teacher is bewitched—
By your new wonderful Genie,
And all your wishes are fulfilled—
By The Intelligent Resourceful Prodigy!

Now that The Prodigy has come to school, I cannot thank her enough,
She has saved many difficult moments for us.
Hiding behind her, we are safe—
From the gruelling schedule at school, we escape!

THE DRAMA PRINCESS

Once upon a time, there was a princess,
Who was kind and content and easy to please—
And once upon a time there was this prince,
Who wanted to find a bride and have a kid.

They married, and amidst their laughter,
Thought that it would mean happy-ever-after—
But even fairy tales have some rotter,
It started when they had their deary daughter.

Their young princess was a greedy lass,
Never satisfied, ever a fuss—
So, the king was quite disgusted,
Still, he tried his best to ignore.

So, when his spoilt daughter came to him and asked,
'Father, can I have a ball gown for the dance?'
He did not object, but sighed and said,
'Call the royal tailor, my dear, right away.'

When the arrogant young lady made a scene,
'Father, you *must* give me a limousine!'
He had no other choice,
Than to order one, with a strangled voice.

When the conceited princess ran up to him and said quite breathless,
'Father, *won't* you give me a real pearl necklace?'
He was forced to again do the same—
'Yes, of course, my dear, as you say.'

This continued for many a tiresome day,
Till the king's nerves were fried and frayed.
'Enough! Enough!' he angrily cried,
'Princess, you are growing worse with time!'

'You are dripping with diamonds, decked like a dance ball,
You wear those heels till you stagger and fall.
You act like you're better than everyone, a big know-it-all—
But you are nothing, my dear, nothing more than a silver spoon doll!'

The princess gazed in astonishment, trying to hide her injured pride,
'But it's my birthday tomorrow!' feeling hurt she cried.
'I want...' she started. 'Oh no,' thought the king as she ploughed on and on—
'It's *such* a small list,' she finished at last, by dawn!

The king had no idea what to do,
He was sure, his royal treasury would be doomed.
His kingdom needed attention—
And here he was, ordering dresses and royal diamonds.

Fed up, he told his wife,
About his dreadful strife.
The queen, who knew how to handle greed—
Smiled and said, 'Just leave it to me.'

She found her daughter, waiting for her gifts,
Went up to her and bestowed a kiss.
'Happy birthday, my dear!' the queen wished—
'Where are my presents?' the princess coldly replied.

'On their way, my dear, on their way,
But I say! You look delightful today!'
'Oh, Mother!' the princess gleefully exclaimed—
'Aren't I the best?' she continued unashamed.

'Oh, you are just like Snow White in your looks,
And you are Cinderella's rival when you dance, I'm sure.
But that's outside; inside, you are so much better!
There's such a colourful and varied persona in my daughter!'

‘What do you mean, Mother?’
‘Oh, my darling, don’t act so modest,
Don’t pretend you don’t know—
That you fit into so many roles.

‘Now, when your father gave you lovely dresses, didn’t you want more?
Doesn’t that remind you of Cinderella’s stepsisters?
And when your father scolded you, weren’t you still adamant?
Like the Evil Queen in Snow White and the Seven Dwarves?

‘When another princess got a pearl necklace, didn’t you want a much better one too?
A streak of Nightshade- so insecure?
And when your father didn’t give you a jazzy new car,
Didn’t you blackmail him just like witty, wicked Scar?

‘Oh, I have been watching you, my princess,
And I know you can be very stubborn and ruthless.
Looks can be deceptive, my love—
Beautiful outside but ugly inside, sweetheart!’

With this, the queen stopped,
And when the princess finally spoke, her voice was choked.
‘I’m sorry, Mother, I really am.’
‘I’ll try my best to be nice now, yes I really can.’

‘I’ll never be vain or mean or silly,
I’ll no longer be greedy.
Will you and father forgive me?’
‘Of course we will,’ the queen said sweetly.

‘But,’ the princess grinned,
‘I had *one* request.
As a good omen, can I have—
Cinderella’s glass slipper or Moana’s jewel necklace?’

‘Well, well,’ Maleficent smirked, then smiled,
‘Some things never change,’ Elsa replied.
Sighed Tinker Bell like a magical bard—
‘Old habits surely die hard.’

INSPIRING INTROSPECTIONS

HOME SWEET HOME

Do you ever wonder why a bird,
Returns to its nest each night:
No matter where it has flown?
Maybe, because it knows—
There's no place like home.

There may be a place a hundred miles north or south,
There may be a place a hundred miles east or west:
Where the breeze may be soothing or the nest comfortable,
Or the sky aglow at sunset:
Where soothing sounds may lull it to rest—
But it still finds its home the best.

Maybe because, the bird knows,
That wherever it goes, it will be known:
Not by where it has settled, but from where it has flown—
Not by where it finds its food, but from where it belongs—
Not by the garden he is in but from where its tree's roots are sown.

Maybe because, the bird knows,
That in storm it will be offered shade:
Not by those chirpy ones around it—
By those who were its caretakers, love-givers,
But by those to whom it was born.

Maybe because, the bird knows,
That when it is without a grain:
It will be welcomed by—
Not its fair-weathered friends, how much ever they beam,
But by its humble home that has both storm and shade seen.

When it has no wing upon which to cry,
When every mate flies by:
When nobody cares to wipe its tear—
To bring him home and support him,
His peaceful abode will always be there.

The eagles, woodpeckers, owls and kingfishers,
Doves, herons, wrens, robins and peacocks:
All follow this rule—
And although Nature has her secrets,
We can only hope this reasoning is true.

One bird, however, likes to be the exception,
The cuckoo neither makes a nest nor nests in one every day.
And sadly, more humans are "cuckooing" out of their homes, every day.

If only they knew what the little birdie knows—
Then they might not have flown.

Because it matters not where they have settled,
But from where they have flown—
Not where they bloom, but where they belong:
Even if they hustle in the world—
A thousand times,
There's no place like home,
Where those roots are sown.

MAGIC, ANYONE ?

I'm a fairy godmother,
Yes, the one you've read about in fairy tales—
I'm the one who's guided every princess,
And shown her how to find the magic in herself.

Yes, I can spell magic,
I can teach you to shine and dazzle—
But you need to make yourself so fantastic,
That you fight your own battles.

So now that every princess has found her prince,
Maybe I can tell you what I taught the trail blazers—
I will tell the world what the pretty pioneers really did,
And why they all have happy-ever-afters.

When you're pushing your carriage of life, but it isn't any quicker,
And you can't be patient and balanced—
When the clock strikes doom, and luck slips like a slipper,
Stay serene, stay virtuous and you will reach your palace.

Even when your family is cold and bitter,
When hatred is the hilt of a sword—
Be true and a good soul, but don't adorn every wall of life with a mirror,
For a poisoned apple has a cure, but not a poisoned soul.

Even if the rose is full of thorns,
When losses are a ritual, don't let any wind of scorn—
Overshadow your candle of intelligence, even a Beast has beauty inside,
Care for others, be humble, brave and kind.

When the magic carpet can't fly you away from animosity,
And a genie can't discern between good and evil—
Speak for yourself, be adventurous, but act cautiously,
Even the best friend can be the worst devil.

When you are trapped in the tower of fright, longing for new beginnings,
Cut away the worry, add curiosity and charity—

When the scissors of longing are tugging at your heartstrings,
Snip away the selfishness, follow your heart's fantasies.

When the needle of despair stings the sharpest,
Stay loyal, stay positive, you can start anew—
When you are cursed, don't dread the fall,
Believe in yourself, don't give up, your dreams will come true.

When snowflakes are swirling on the horizon,
And the glove of restraint is imprisoning your bold hand—
Be free and independent, embrace your differences, be your own sun,
Keep your heart warm, even if you are a snowman.

But, dear dreamer, you must keep in mind,
I'm none other than your inner voice, your guiding light—
For today, while there are no wands or gowns to reach your goal,
Believe in yourself, for the fairy godmother is within your soul!

Now that you know the secret of their magic,
Do you think you can find yours?
You may be the next Snow White or Belle, who knows?
Never stop dreaming, and the world is yours!

TALES

THE URGE TO BELONG

'Hey, look who's here!' announced the first, her voice dripping with sarcasm.

'The girl with no phone, no friends!' mocked the second callously.

'No wonder her mother is afraid… she might get thrown out any day!'

Eisha jerked upright, opening her eyes, as the bus came to a shuddering halt. She picked up her bag and walked towards the door. She tried to ignore the pointed stares of all the girls and the slight sniggering around her, as if she was a walking talking caricature. She tried to forget what she'd heard in her dream, but it wasn't easy, because their laughter kept reminding her of it.

She heard them roaring with laughter as she climbed down the steps. She turned her back against them, rudely, hoping they'd take the hint and stop.

But their guffaws doubled, and she could see a few of them rolling in their seats. She looked away, angrily.

For a thirteen-year-old, Eisha was very tall and lanky. She had dark brown eyes with a fair complexion. Her brown curls with short fringes dancing on her broad forehead made her look messy at times. She looked pretty when she smiled but it was a rare sight.

I can't understand what they're finding so funny about me. Is there something wrong with my hair? Is there something strange on my back?

On a hunch, she put her hand up to her back and wasn't surprised to find a piece of paper pinned there. It read, 'Misfit ready for expulsion?'

She turned to look at their faces, but the bus was gone. She could still hear their laughter.

I hate them, she thought, grumpily, as she trudged up the stairs to her house, *they only do it to poke fun at me and make me feel miserable.*

Eisha sighed, fishing a key from her bag.

Why doesn't anyone like me? Why am I always alone- both at school and at home? Am I going to be expelled? Is Mum scared that I won't last long in school? Why does everything have to always go wrong with me?

She put the key in the lock and turned it.

I should stop dozing in the bus, she thought, it's just my dreams that keep haunting me. But I hope my life won't become a nightmare.

She opened the door.

Or will it?

....

Twenty minutes later, a tall woman wearing a long scarf slipped the key into the lock and entered her house. She looked exhausted, windswept and famished.

Eisha, still in her uniform, shoved some books over a mobile phone on which a game was beeping, then unlocked the door of her room and came out, annoyance written large on her face.

'Why didn't you pack something better for lunch?' she asked irritably.

‘Sorry, dear, I got late this morning… Did you have a good day?’

‘Just a lot worse than utterly pathetic,’ muttered Eisha, in a typical teenager tone. She was hoping the phone wouldn’t beep and give the game away, literally.

‘Why haven’t you changed yet, Eisha?’

‘I just came half a minute ago,’ muttered Eisha, trying to hide her red face. ‘I need to do something important now, don’t disturb me.’

‘Wait.’

Eisha saw her mother looking at her with unmistakable concern. She had undone her scarf, to reveal a kindly, firm and stern woman. She looked like she could counsel fifty misbehaving adolescents but could also be the “cool” mom at a teenagers’ party. You couldn’t cross the line with her, but you couldn’t help trusting her, either.

At that moment, however, she gave her daughter a look that could’ve cowed a bull. Eisha sat down on a chair facing her, feeling terrified. Caught in the quicksand of her own lies, she was struggling to find solid ground. Yet, seeing the fear and remorse in Eisha’s eyes, her mother’s anger seemed to quite melt away.

‘I don’t get much time after work, Eisha, but is there anything bothering you? Anything you want?’ Her mother asked her gently.

'No, of course there's nothing worthwhile *you* can get me. And anyways, your *work* isn't the most elite profession in the world. Anyone can be a snappy supervisor,' she said, cockily; her sarcasm restored.

'You know I don't like disrespectful children, and definitely not my own child,' her mother said coldly. Her tone softened and she gave Eisha a deeper look. 'What is wrong? I know something is, so tell me, won't you? I am quite experienced in handling such issues, you know...'

'Yes, of course you're experienced!' interrupted Eisha, 'How can I forget, with you telling me so every hour of every day of every week?' She took a deep breath. 'All the girls say that you're afraid I'll be thrown out...' her voice trailed away as she realized what she'd said.

'Eisha, how could you? You...' her mother faltered, searching for words 'You think I'd want my own daughter to be expelled from school?'

'I'm sorry...' Eisha said trying to make amends, but her mother had lost her temper, and she turned away, angrily.

'Go to your room, Eisha, and think about what you've said. Only speak to me at dinner, after you've had time to turn things over in your mind.'

Eisha had no option but to submit.

Furious with everyone, Eisha paced up and down. She sat down on her bed and stared at the note that had been stuck on her back in the bus, a part of the unkind "practical" joke.

She turned it over, dully.

Then she saw what was written on the back of the note, and her eyes wandered to the rough stack of books in the corner, not meant for studying, but for camouflaging her deceit from her mother and a funny sensation tickled her eyes and her throat as her vision grew blurry. The note seemed to melt in her hands.

....

Had Eisha already believed that the day was one of the most depressing ones?

The worst was yet to come.

At the dinner table, Eisha apologised to her mother, but she couldn't resist blurting out what was bothering her.

'All my friends have phones, except me. They all have chat groups and social networking accounts. They all fit in, they all *belong*, but I don't. And I probably never will.'

Her mother sighed deeply. 'If this is what it means to "belong", then trust me, Eisha, it's not as important to "belong", as it is to be focused and safe.

I've often told you that it does not matter if you have ten friends or two, because you'll always have me. And phones aren't for children...

'Yeah, alright,' said Eisha, "I knew you'd say that. You're so overprotective and old school. You don't care if I remain a misfit all my life, as long as I don't get a phone. You asked me if there's something I'd like, and this is that something, but you don't want to give it to me. Is it too much to ask for? Don't I deserve friends?'

'Eisha, what insolence!' her mother exclaimed. 'I thought you just apologised.'

'Sorry. Honestly, talking to you is like begging the vice principal for a holiday, and there isn't much difference between the two. I'm going to bed.'

The next morning, Eisha felt downcast. She had been strictly denied a mobile phone and thought she would be lonely for years, with no friends. Instead of an understanding and loving mother, she had one who would lose no opportunity to berate her daughter for the slightest peccadillo. To make matters worse, her mother was on an all-consuming, relentless anti-mobile-phones-for-little-children campaign!

But the tide was soon going to change.

'You will get a phone, but it has to be strictly used for school communication and schoolwork ONLY', the words felt like music to her ears. Her heart leaped with joy. 'Finally,' she mumbled.

'I trust you, Eisha,' her mother said, as she dropped her off to school, never betray that trust, and I'll always stand by you.'

Eisha nodded, but the words she'd read yesterday, at the back of the note, were throwing her mind into a turmoil…

"Get a phone, and maybe you'll get a friend... misfit! Don't say we didn't warn you."

....

A week had passed since Eisha's mother had granted her permission to use a phone as her own, which had once been Eisha's father's old phone. Her mother had been surprised to find numerous games and social media applications already cluttering the phone when she had first given it to Eisha but fortunately for the latter, she overlooked it. Eisha could have kicked herself for not deleting the apps before her mother got her hands on the phone. But luckily (or unluckily), her mother was unsuspecting that her daughter's sneaky behaviour had begun even before she got the phone.

That day, she'd shown off her prized possession to her newly emerged group of five friends, who were all daughters of teachers in the school. The girls in the group mocked all their teachers, including their mothers, and Eisha joined in this derision. This, coupled with her allowance to use a phone, added to her popularity.

Whenever Eisha sat with them, she felt a happy glow inside her, the wonderful joy that came with the feeling of finally *"belonging"*. The friends in the group only referred to each other by their groovy nicknames, and Eisha had been given the nickname Ash.

Even Minya (aka"Mi"), who often cold-shouldered Eisha, agreed that it was a 'cool' name.

All had their own phones.

They'd sit together in the lunch break and discuss the general gossip from all over the school. Eisha was certain she didn't want any teacher to hear, least of all the formidable vice principal.

One day, as they were deep in discussion about Mi's latest brainwave to create their own chat group, the vice principal herself happened to stroll by.

Ash stiffened, her heart racing as if caught red-handed. Mi, on the other hand, smirked with a mischievous glint in her eye that left Ash bewildered.

The vice principal cast them a curious glance, but then, to their immense relief, continued on her way.

After that, the girls were cautious and only discussed their plans when there was no teacher within earshot. Although Mi sometimes spoke and laughed rather too loudly, especially when the vice principal was around.

At home, Ash checked her phone and found that the chat group had been made and she was the admin. Many messages were waiting for her, and she trembled in anticipation.

What fun!

Another week flew by, and Eisha was living a double

life—superstar Ash at school and unassuming Eisha at home. She revelled in the thrill of her secret. Did her mother catch on? Not a chance. Eisha's elaborate pretence remained intact, and she felt invincible.

....

Another week later, one Monday morning, the vice principal walked to the group during the brunch break. She looked grim. "Come to my office at once, Eisha."

Her tone was ominous. Ash had a sense of foreboding.

What *could have* happened?

Once in office, the vice principal gave Ash a look that could've cowed a bull.

'Eisha, I have come to know that you are part of a chat group in which you all heavily troll the teachers. You are in this group with four teachers, who are extremely upset by your antics and have reported to me. *Explain yourself.*'

'I think you are mistaken, I… I am in the group with four of my friends, you saw them sitting with me just now.'

'No, your chat group has teachers!'

'But… but…' Eisha stammered, 'there seems to be some misunderstanding … they're surely my friends! You can even check their profile pictures!'

'The profile pictures are of the teacher's daughters. Minya, your friend, persuaded the rest of your group to coax their mothers to change the pictures, just before adding you to the chat. They decided to play this rather cruel "practical" prank on you. I don't know if you would call them your enemies, but they are certainly not your friends.'

Eisha could scarcely breathe.

'Owing to the content you uploaded online, where you have taken digs at teachers and the fact that you are the admin of the group, I will have to…'

She took a deep breath, '…expel you.'

The teacher's face had been like a mask all this time, but it was starting to crack.

'There was time, Eisha, when you were Eisha, and not Ash. There was a time, Eisha, when I could have helped you, if you had only asked. You were given the phone, given the liberty to do as you liked, but most of all, you had your mother's trust, and you gave it all away in the allure of a few fake friends. You forgot you had a friend in your very home who was always there for you. I am sorry, Eisha, and truly embarrassed, by what you have done.

But now, whatever you have to say will amount to nothing. You may leave now and spend your last afternoon on this campus.'

The vice principal's office, with its polished wooden desk and the scent of freshly brewed coffee, seemed to echo her words with a stern, unwavering authority. The sunlight filtering through the blinds cast striped shadows on the floor, adding to the atmosphere of discipline and order.

Eisha walked towards the door, her head hanging low in shame. Just as she reached for the handle, the teacher's voice sliced the silence.

'Eisha!'

Her heart pounded as she turned, tears falling fast and unchecked down her cheeks. The teacher struggled to meet her gaze, and Eisha could barely lift her eyes.

'I won't be home early today', the teacher began, her voice wavering, 'I have to supervise the concert practice. I needed to inform you, in case you… wouldn't want to use the phone anymore...'

Time seemed to stand still. The teacher's words hung heavy in the air. She looked at Eisha for a long, tear-jerking moment. Her eyes glistening with unshed tears, she could barely speak.

'Happy Daughters' Day, Eisha.'

PARVATI

Twelve-year-old Parvati was an obedient and smart girl who lived in a quaint village bordering Maharashtra and Karnataka. Her mother had died when she was very young, and she had been brought up single-handedly by her father. They spoke both Marathi and Kannada, and sometimes she got confused between the two languages!

Parvati was named after her namesake, the brave and beautiful goddess, Parvati, whom her mother had deeply revered. Her mother believed that children are a form of God, a belief her father often reminded her of.

But, despite being witty, talented, and sincere, Parvati lacked the goddess-like charm. Her dark skin, wide-set eyes, and pointed chin made her the subject of ridicule among her friends and some relatives, who called her "Bhayānaka" instead of Parvati, which means "terrible" in Kannada. This resulted in the sensible, understanding girl becoming quite under-confident and impatient.

Nevertheless, Parvati did not lose heart at most times and put up a brave front. One day, during a fair organized in her village, all the children made fun of her looks as she passed by. Parvati did not break down but boldly held her head high, remembering the goddess she had been named after. Her father had often told her that it did not matter what others said because he knew that she was beautiful.

The lowest point for Parvati came when she mistakenly thought her father had called her by her loathed nickname, "Bhayānaka" when he was actually saying she was "bahumulya" (precious) in Marathi!

This misunderstanding was the last straw for the young girl who had lost faith in everyone except her father. And she had now lost faith in him, too.

Feeling overwhelmed and immensely hurt, Parvati fled from home in a sudden fit of fury, intending to return once her anger subsided. However, upon her return, she found no sign of her father and felt certain he wasn't even bothered about her. Parvati's rage reared like a snake. She set out in a huff, and only stopped when she reached the small Shiva temple a few miles north of their village.

She had always loved and revered the great God Shiva and his wife. Driven by pure devotion, Parvati took on the anonymous identity of Annapurna, a manifestation of the Goddess Parvati Herself, and settled in the small village.

She sold flowers, coconuts, garlands, sweets, and other offerings for the temple. Over time, she began working in the temple itself, cleaning and caring for the Shiva Linga. She slept in a small quarter at the back of the temple and earned enough money for her meals.

Almost a week had passed, and despite finding contentment in her new surroundings, Parvati couldn't help missing her father.

But unbeknownst to her, her father had been desperately searching for her in all the nearby villages. Worried and anxious, he first visited a wise old sage who lived on the outskirts of their village and sought his help.

'Do not worry, you will find her. Go to the place where her name is chanted, where you think she would be happy. And do not forget to assure her that you are always there for her,' advised the sage.

And so, guided by this advice, the distraught father went off in search of his daughter. One evening, he reached a small village. Tired, he was about to rest when he saw a Shiva temple. An inner voice told him to go in, he felt an instinctual pull that his daughter might be close by, and he stepped inside.

That night, Parvati was sleeping at the back of the temple as usual, when she suddenly awoke to the sound of footsteps. Wondering who could be in the temple at that late hour, she quietly crept outside. Finding no one, she was about to leave when she heard the sound again; this time it seemed to come from within the temple. Holding her breath, Parvati made her way to the *garbagriha*, or main shrine of the temple.

Just as she found her way to the garbagriha in the dark, she tripped over a pair of feet! Astonished, she was about to ask who it was, when she heard—

'Who are you and why have you come here in the dark?'

Parvati replied calmly, 'I am Parvati.'

Parvati had forgotten that she was supposed to call herself Annapurna, who was also coincidentally a manifestation of the Goddess Parvati Herself!

The man's response was quite unexpected. He did not speak for a while, and when he did, his voice was weak and trembling.

'O Goddess! I am blessed to see you. I am so sorry to have come inside the garbagriha at this odd hour. Please forgive me, Oh divine Goddess.'

It was then that it dawned on Parvati that the man had mistaken her for the real Goddess Parvati! Even though she could have told him that he was mistaken, she did not do so, not at that moment, at least.

So, she played along, and said in what she hoped was a Goddess-like voice.

'Do not worry, may you be blessed and happy.'

Then, feeling that she had overdone the Goddess act, she was about to leave when she realized that the man had just given a dry sob. She couldn't leave him and go! She gently asked him what was troubling him.

'O Goddess,' he replied, sobbing harder than ever now. 'My only daughter has left the house, and I can't find her! I came here because I knew she worshipped Shiva and Parvati, but with no luck. Please help me.'

'Yes, of course, do not worry,' replied Parvati in a composed manner, but her heart was heavy.

She watched the man stumble back out of the temple. Without an iota of doubt, she knew that he was her father. And he had considered her to be a Goddess in the temple of Parvati.

She made her way to her chamber in the dark, her heart heavy. She knew she had to do something but pondered over what to do.

She wondered why he hadn't guessed that she was his daughter, despite revealing her name to him.

She lay down and fell into an uncomfortable slumber.

The next night she decided to go and wait for her father to return.

He did. He clearly revered her as a Goddess. He told her of how he had visited the sage, how much he loved his daughter and how much he was worried about her safety. Hearing his deep sorrow and longing for his daughter, Parvati realized she had misunderstood him and felt sad.

Parvati made up her mind. Her anger had melted, and she decided to reveal herself to her father the next day.

But the morning brought a huge surprise for Parvati. There was a lot of hustle-bustle in and around the temple. The village was abuzz with some rumour. And then Parvati heard the news that had spread like wildfire all through the village. An incarnation of Goddess Parvati had graced the temple last night! A man who had visited the temple at midnight had told everyone of his experience of meeting the Goddess in person.

Parvati was dumbstruck to hear this. Just as she was about to reveal her true identity to her father, the whole village was eager to meet the Goddess!

Her first thought was to spill the beans and inform the village folk of what had actually taken place over the last two nights. But then another thought soon crossed her mind. Was it possible that an incarnation of Goddess was visiting the temple each night? Perhaps she would do so today, too? If so, she ought to wait for her, tonight, just like all the other villagers.

That night, the entire village waited in the temple until late midnight. The small Shiva temple glowed with the soft light of oil lamps, their flames dancing with a divine glow. Marigold garlands adorned the stone walls, and the scent of incense wafted through the air, creating an aura of sacred serenity. The throng entered the temple's garbagriha from the front door, while Parvati slipped in through the back door, behind which her small quarters were. In the pitch darkness near the back of the garbagriha, only her silhouette was visible.

Suddenly, the chanting of 'Parvati Devi Namah', 'Shakti Devi Namah', and 'All praise be to the divine and beautiful Goddess' filled the silence of the night. Parvati, eager to witness the Goddess, stepped forward into the light.

The temple bells rang out, and the people offered her flowers and sought her blessings.

Parvati was stunned. What a muddle she had gotten herself into!

And the most perplexing part was the fact that her own father was completely convinced that she was a goddess in disguise!

Parvati could have revealed her identity, but she did not wish to undermine the villagers' faith in the Goddess. She spoke to them in a godly voice:

'Oh, my children. I am so happy to see you all here. I have seen the trouble you have taken to stay up all night and decorate the entire temple! I am pleased with you. But there is one problem. You see, the man who first saw me in this temple has lost his daughter. I know that she was upset because everyone called her ugly. Now, I have come in her simple human form to the temple, and you all call me divine and beautiful! I don't understand this. Can you tell me why this is so?'

Parvati paused, and the villagers were left baffled. She continued in a gentler tone, 'The important thing for everyone to know is that beauty is not the yardstick to judge others. Everyone is beautiful, just as they are! The way you perceive beauty in others shows just how beautiful you are! Should you judge anyone based on their appearances? For that matter, you are all my children, and to me, all of you are beautiful. Just remember, 'beauty lies in the eyes of the beholder.''

Each word made sense to the villagers. They listened to her intently. Parvati continued-

'Tomorrow night, the little girl's father will find her outside the temple. I am always there in your hearts even if you may not see me again in a human form. May you all live in love and peace!'

With that, Parvati left, and the chanting in the praise of the Goddess continued till dawn.

The next night, outside the temple, under a sky sprinkled with a million twinkling stars and bathed in the silvery glow of the moon, Parvati's father saw his daughter clearly. His heart pounded with a mixture of relief and disbelief, and tears streamed down his face. Parvati stood frozen, unable to move as she watched her father approach.

'Oh father!' Parvati cried out, her voice breaking with emotion.

Her father's steps faltered as he reached her, and he fell to his knees, overwhelmed. 'Parvati, my precious Parvati,' he whispered, his voice trembling. 'I cannot believe I found you. I am so thankful to the Goddess. She has brought back my little Goddess Parvati.'

'But didn't you call me "Bhayānaka", father?' Parvati's tears flowed freely; her voice filled with years of pent-up pain.

Her father looked up at her, his eyes filled with sorrow and love. 'Oh, my dear Parvati, do you for one instance believe that you are less than a Goddess to me? You are so bahumulya (precious) to me. Can your father ever call you "Bhayānaka"?'

With trembling hands, he reached out and touched her face. 'You are all I have, Parvati, and I cannot tell you how much it pained me to see my little Goddess leave me like this. You are always the most beautiful one to me; you are always bahumulya, the most precious one! Never leave me like this again, Parvati. For my child, you are the most valuable gift of Goddess Parvati to me.'

He lifted her up in his arms, his grip strong and protective. They clung to each other, their hearts overflowing with love and relief. As they embraced, the temple bells suddenly rang out, their clear, resonant tones filling the air. The sound seemed to echo the divine approval of their reunion.

The villagers, witnessing this powerful moment, began to chant with renewed fervour, 'All praise to the divine and beautiful Goddess!'

In that instant, under the watchful eyes of the moon and stars, Parvati and her father felt a sense of peace and joy embrace them. The night brimmed with divine energy, as if the Goddess herself blessed the father and his precious daughter.

Parvati's father, still holding her tightly, whispered, 'This moment, my beloved daughter, is a miracle. It is a gift from the Goddess. We are home.'

Parvati nodded, tears of joy streaming down her face. 'Yes, father... we are home.'

A BAG-CHECK

The last day of school was always a riot of excitement for the students. They surged through the hallways like a burst of confetti, their laughter echoing off the walls, as the promise of holidays waved at them from just beyond the horizon. The air buzzed with their eagerness to leave behind the confines of the classroom.

For the teachers, however, the scene was quite different. As the students rushed out, they remained anchored to their desks, facing the daunting mountain of exam papers that awaited correction. The holidays, though visible in the distance, felt like a mirage, tantalisingly close yet still out of reach. The teachers braced themselves for the uphill climb.

But before that, the students' last day bag-checks were carried out, a last day ritual in the school. The intention was to ensure that the children reached home safely after the last day of school, and did not sneak out with friends without their parents' knowledge. The prefects, vice-prefects, head girl, and vice-head girl oversaw the activity with a keen eye. They had to make sure that nobody carried any casual clothes in their bags with the motive of changing on the way and partying off with a friend instead of going home. They also had to ensure that no one carried any prohibited items like cosmetics or electronics. Each bag was scrutinised as if it held secrets, the students' nervous whispers and occasional laughter punctuating the air. But amidst the organised chaos, the head girl seemed to have disappeared, just when she was most needed to supervise this crucial exercise.

'I last saw her in the staff room when I went in there before the principal's address,' said the history teacher, her brows furrowing in thought. 'I asked her why she was there, and she mumbled something about getting Geography papers. But then, why would she be rummaging through some teacher's bag? Strange!'

'I saw her checking the bags that were lying outside the auditorium when the principal was speaking. I was slightly late, and there she was, snooping around the bags!' said the biology teacher, her eyes narrowing with suspicion.

'I suppose she's lurking in some fourth-grade classroom and checking those little kids' bags for weapons when she knows she ought to be here,' said the art mistress, her voice dripping with her usual exaggeration.

'I guess she takes her orders too seriously,' said the vice principal, as the teachers reported this to her. 'She's a new girl in the school this year and has never really overseen a bag-check before. She goes by the book though! And I told her to make sure nobody, and I *meant* NOBODY was carrying things that weren't allowed.'

Meanwhile, in the staff room, the task of correcting answer sheets had already begun, now that all the students had gone home, save for one or two prefects, the vice head-girl, and the head girl, who were supposed to stay back for an hour to help the teachers and staff with the winding up. The room was a hive of activity, filled with the rustle of papers and the murmur of conversations. Bundles of papers lay stacked precariously on tables, several balanced on chairs, and many more stuffed in bags, waiting their turn, as teachers settled in for the long haul.

The correction expedition would take nearly two weeks, a daunting task that loomed over them like a mountain to be climbed. The teachers knew they would have to come to school each day until the last paper was graded, which would take a couple of weeks. The staff room, usually a place of respite, had transformed into a battlefield of intellect and perseverance, where each corrected answer sheet was a small victory.

'Has anyone seen my drawings?' asked Mrs. Kothari, the art teacher, hurrying around, in a dither. Her usually merry demeanour was now replaced with anxious flutters. 'Oh, I do hope the prefects haven't placed them in some wrong pile.' The staff room seemed to mirror her unease as she moved from chairs to tables.

'Why, what would they do, confiscate them?' joked the chemistry teacher, who had just finished one of her bundles and was quite in the mood to celebrate.

'I would believe the head girl Rebecca could even go for a teacher's bag-check! A proper teacher's pet, who has the audacity to trespass into our space too! I'm sure I saw her near the staff room cupboard this morning, probably trying to rummage through a teacher's belongings! Quite unacceptable!' The indignation in her voice hung in the air, freezing the atmosphere of the room slowly. The usual hum of activity ceased, as everyone collectively held their breath, the tension in the room was palpable.

The geography teacher, Mrs. Jones, suddenly looked up and spoke sharply to the art teacher. 'You needn't worry so much. She had just come here to fetch the geography exam paper's solution sheet for me. The grade seven answer sheet, not grade ten,' she added hastily, as Mrs. Kothari opened her mouth to object.

'Well, whatever you may say, I personally would believe anything of that girl. And what I'd like to know now, is where are my drawings?'

'I'm not surprised you lost them. You probably misplaced them yourself—it would be the fiftieth time this week. I don't know how your students tolerate your absent-mindedness! Honestly, I'm glad you're not my student. If you were…'

‘I’d drive you absolutely bonkers!’ finished Mrs. Kothari, with a laugh. ‘And for the record, my dear ma’am, you probably said that for the one hundredth time! I don’t know how your students tolerate your endlessly repetitive instructive lectures… they must be having the patience of saints!’

‘And I don’t know how your students keep up with your *artistic* chaos!’ retorted the geography teacher. ‘They must have the agility of circus performers to dodge your misplaced supplies!’

‘Thank you, Mrs. Jones,’ said the art teacher starchily. The staff room, filled with the scent of old books and the quiet hum of the ceiling fan, seemed to pause for a moment. The stacks of papers and the distant sounds of the school grounds outside created a backdrop of subdued activity, contrasting with the flux of conversation and silence.

The other teachers returned to their work. Their bittersweet friendship was known to one and all, swinging like an oscillating pendulum in the physics laboratory, between camaraderie and rivalry.

Just then, as the clock struck two, three teachers came bustling in, their arms piled high with papers and books that would dominate their lives for the next two weeks. Yet, amidst the scholarly mayhem, they also held peculiar items that told tales of their own. Wonky hats tilted precariously, funky glasses perched at odd angles, a pair of ripped jeans flung over a shoulder like a fashion statement gone rogue. A couple of humorous caricatures peeped out from the top of the stack, their exaggerated features eliciting quiet chuckles.

One teacher gripped a Christmas cap adorned with pigtails that flashed with tiny, multicoloured lights, which would make anyone look like an eccentric holiday elf. Titbits of papers fluttered to the ground like rebellious snowflakes, while a brightly coloured file with a psychedelic pattern seemed almost too cheerful for the mundane task at hand. Other curiosities jostled for space, each with its own story, turning the entrance into a parade of academic absurdity.

'More papers?' asked the middle-school physics teacher, Mrs. Abel, with a sympathetic sigh. She was in a relentless battle with her own towering stack of assignments, which seemed to multiply overnight like gremlins.

'Yes, I'm afraid so,' sighed the maths teacher, Mrs. Punia, her glasses slipping down her nose. 'But there's also a surprise hidden in this load, if you care to look for it.' She tapped the pile with a mysterious smile, as if it might reveal a treasure map at any moment.

'Won't you come out for a bit, Abel?' chimed in Mrs. Verma, the hindi teacher, with a twinkle in her eye. 'We can reveal it to you there.' She motioned dramatically towards the door, as if they were about to escape to Wonderland, and frankly, to Abel, it felt *just* like that.

'No, I've got loads of work yet, I'm sorry, I can't...'

'By Newton's apple!' exclaimed Mrs. Abel, as her eyes fell on the quirky Christmas cap. 'Where in the universe of thermodynamics did you find that?'

The other teachers laughed, their laughter ringing through the room like a merry bell chorus. Mrs. Sushmita, the English teacher who had also come in, said lightly, 'I think correcting papers is having a bad effect on you, Abel.

Anyway, do take a break and come outside to have a chat over a cup of tea. And of course, these oddities.'

'If you insist,' said Abel, relenting, and gladly making her way to the shady trees near the basketball court. The sun filtered through the leaves, creating a dappled pattern on the ground, and the air was filled with the scent of freshly brewed tea and warm snacks.

'So where *did* you find them?' Abel finally asked, as the other three began discussing exam paper corrections, the upcoming report card day, and the classes they were likely to teach next year. All four were middle-school teachers, and despite all their moaning and groaning over the strenuous work they were expected to do, they all had a soft spot in their hearts for the sixth and seventh graders.

'Now that is interesting, isn't it?' smiled Mrs. Punia, settling herself comfortably under the tree's shade. She patted the ground beside her, encouraging the others to join her. 'We found them in the long wooden cupboard in the main staffroom. We helped the ancillary staff clean it, and lo and behold, we found these treasures!'

The others burst into laughter, imagining the scene. 'Oh, I can just see you, Sushmita, pulling out that Christmas cap with pigtails!' Mrs. Abel said, clutching her sides. 'It must have been quite the discovery!'

'Yes, it was like stumbling upon a hidden relic,' Mrs. Sushmita added, with an amused chuckle. 'You never know what you might find in that old cupboard.'

The group chuckled softly, the stress of their workload momentarily easing.

'Indeed,' smiled Abel.

Everyone - teachers, students, and staff - knew that the wooden cupboard was the place where the forbidden, confiscated items were stored. "Illegal stuff," as the students referred to it. But for as long as Abel could remember, no one had ever cleaned it out.

'Yes,' said Punia, thoroughly enjoying the excitement this news had caused. 'Interesting, isn't it?'

With a flourish, she began to display the oddities, turning the tea break into an impromptu show-and-tell.

'Hmm... wait - what's this?' Mrs. Abel asked, gesturing towards something that looked like sunglasses, except that one lens was circular and the other was diamond shaped. They were so brightly coloured that they seemed to bend the light around them, casting a prismatic glow.

'Sunglasses, of course! Though I must admit that I have never seen anything like these!' chuckled Mrs. Punia.

The teachers exchanged amused glances. Mrs. Verma chuckled. 'Those must have been quite the fashion statement back in the day!'

Mrs. Sushmita nodded, her eyes twinkling with amusement, 'You never know what treasures you'll find in that cupboard. It's like a time capsule of school contraband.'

'The person who owned these, surely wanted to become a rockstar!' added Sushmita.

'Crazy!' chortled Mrs. Verma.

Mrs. Abel laughed in agreement. Suddenly, her eyes fell on the torn jeans. They had been over-ripped in a way that made them look exaggerated, almost theatrical. Somehow, the vibrant hues of the jeans seemed to gel perfectly with the outrageous sunglasses.

'Look at these jeans!' exclaimed Mrs. Sushmita, holding them up, envisioning the bold student who once carried these. 'You'd need a lot of confidence to pull off this ensemble.'

'Must have been quite the character!', chuckled Mrs. Punia.

'Are these the rockstar's too?' asked Abel, pointing at the jeans.

'Obviously!' said Sushmita

The teachers shared another round of laughter, imagining

the daring fashionista who had owned the quirky items.

As Abel was contemplating these funky things, Punia picked up a file and, after glancing at it, opened it, with a laugh.

Inside, there were lots of paper slips with humorous caricatures lying higgledy-piggledy.

'What a mess!' gasped Sushmita as she picked up a slip and looked at it. Her eyes widened, her mouth fell open. Then instantaneously, she burst into peals of laughter.

'What's drawn?' demanded Mrs. Punia, picking it up herself. She too, burst into chiming laughter.

Abel picked up the slip to see for herself.

On it, there was a rough caricature made with a red pen, resembling a teacher and a student. The teacher was apparently reprimanding the student. The figures were very crudely drawn, so that their features seemed exaggerated and blunt, however, Abel could easily recognise the distinct figure of the head girl, Rebecca, as she stared at an empty sheet in the art class. Underneath was written-

"Teacher: Why aren't you drawing, Rebecca?

Rebecca: Ma'am, I *am* drawing. I'm drawing a blank!"

'Oh dear,' giggled Abel 'and look, the others are just as worse. In most of them, the teachers are having fun at the students' expense, not the other way round.'

'If any student had made them, I'd have their stripes for it, but as it's not, well, let's just laugh it away, it's disrespectful for the teachers, I know, but also funny somehow,' said the English teacher.

'It's priceless, and all the caricatures are so exaggerated. Just like the person who made them,' chuckled Punia.

Abel looked blank for a second; she hadn't followed the two teachers' conversation. Then Verma picked up the Christmas cap and, placing it gingerly on her head, stroked the pigtails on it and laughed. Suddenly, the cap flashed coloured lights, and before the astonished teacher knew what was happening, it burst into song.

'We wish you a merry Christmas, we wish you a merry Christmas, we wish you a merry Christmas and a happy new year!' the cap exclaimed joyfully.

The other teachers couldn't help laughing at Mrs. Verma's flummoxed face as she pulled off the cap. Then she joined in the laughter too.

'Well, that was unexpected,' she said finally.

They sipped tea for a couple of minutes in silence, enjoying the peaceful moment. Then Punia glanced at her watch with a sigh. 'I think we need to get going now. We've been here for nearly half an hour, and those papers won't correct themselves.'

‘Are you sure? Maybe they’ve learnt to self-grade by now,’ joked Sushmita.

‘Well, I’m glad we took some time off, though. It’s lightened my mind a bit,’ smiled Abel.

‘Ah, mine too,’ said Sushmita, getting to her feet and dusting off her dress. The teachers gathered their things, the laughter and unexpected joy from their impromptu tea break lingering in the air. As they walked back, Abel couldn’t help but think about the colourful sunglasses, the torn jeans, and the singing cap—all reminders that despite the chaos, a small dose of fun and laughter can work wonders.

‘We must remember to give out the items to the teachers. The games teacher might be interested in the sunglasses and jeans, especially because they match his whistle and cap so much. Mrs. Kothari may be impressed with the caricatures. And the music teacher will be amused to have the cap for the next Christmas choir!’ Sushmita’s voice stirred Abel out of her reverie.

‘The next time I see that wooden cupboard in the staff room, I’ll smile, thinking of all these confiscated things. I’m so glad they decided to clean it at last,’ said Punia.

‘Why did they decide to clean it after an eternity?’ Abel asked, her curiosity piqued.

‘Oh, didn’t you already know? Mr. Sharma lost his glasses, Mrs. Mendoza her Christmas cap, and Mrs. Kothari needed her artwork,’ Sushmita said with a mischievous grin, as if revealing a secret. Mrs. Abel looked baffled, and Mrs. Sushmita leaned in closer, her voice dropping to a conspiratorial whisper.

'Why, you didn't think the students would have the nerve to bring these things to school, did you? It's the teachers who're at it!'

Abel's eyes widened as the realization sank in, that even the strictest of teachers can have surprising backstories. They watched Mrs. Kothari go off with Mrs. Jones; both were laughing hysterically.

On the way to the staffroom, Mrs. Kothari glanced at the items in their arms and called out to the others: 'Rebecca was certainly on the prowl then, wasn't she? I don't know when she checked our bags, but I'm glad she didn't find the caricature I've made of her. If she did, oh dear, I would be expelled!'

They all roared with laughter.

With that, they headed back to their work, hearts a bit lighter, knowing that even amid their busy schedules, moments of unexpected joy and laughter awaited discovery… sometimes in the most unlikely places, like an old wooden cupboard filled with quirky treasures.

Just then, the vice-principal leaned out from the seventh-grade balcony and saw Mrs. Jones and Mrs. Kothari chortling. Realizing that the Head Girl Rebecca had unknowingly conducted a teacher's bag-check, thinking she was confiscating students' items or possibly misinterpreting the instructions given to her, the vice-principal couldn't help but marvel at the unpredictability of both teachers and students.

'Erratic enough to have a student confiscate teachers' belonging!' she thought aloud, startling the Head Girl who was passing by.

'Sorry Ma'am, did you say something to me?' Rebecca asked, but the vice-principal just smiled.

What a funny school this is, thought Rebecca, shaking her head as she finally left the school premises for the holidays.

'Do they think I am crazy enough to conduct a bag-check for the teachers?

As she walked away, Rebecca couldn't help but chuckle at the absurdity of the situation.

Meanwhile, the vice-principal, still amused by the day's events, muttered to herself, 'Well, at least they weren't the students' items this time.'

Back in the staffroom, the teachers shared one last laugh over their unexpected afternoon, each secretly grateful for the comic relief. And as they returned to their duties, the old wooden cupboard stood as a silent testament to the delightful chaos that made their school a place of unexpected joy and camaraderie.

ABOUT THE WRITER

Aarna Khivasara is a student at St. Mary's School, Pune. She has been an avid reader from childhood and the love for reading has translated into penning down her own imagination in the form of poems and stories.

This is Aarna's second book after her maiden attempt at writing the book, *The Little Things in Life: A Pocketful of Poems*.

Writing is Aarna's passion, and she thoroughly enjoys the process. It is for the sheer joy of sharing her creativity that we present her work to you all.

If you like her attempt, do encourage her by writing to her at–
aarna.khivasara@gmail.com

www.ingramcontent.com/pod-product-compliance
Lightning Source LLC
LaVergne TN
LVHW041123150826
845673LV00007B/2166

* 9 7 9 8 8 9 6 3 2 6 4 3 4 *